This Little Tiger book belongs

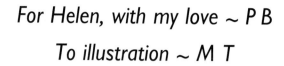

For Helen, with my love ~ P B

To illustration ~ M T

LITTLE TIGER PRESS LTD,
an imprint of the Little Tiger Group
1 Coda Studios, 189 Munster Road, London SW6 6AW
Imported into the EEA by Penguin Random House Ireland,
Morrison Chambers, 32 Nassau Street, Dublin D02 YH68
www.littletiger.co.uk

First published in Great Britain 2009
This edition published 2017

Text copyright © Paul Bright 2009
Illustrations copyright © Michael Terry 2009
Paul Bright and Michael Terry have asserted their rights to be identified as the author
and illustrator of this work under the Copyright, Designs and Patents Act, 1988

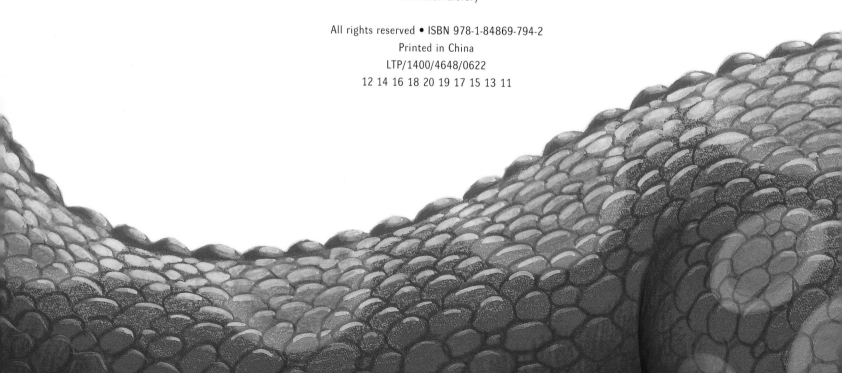

CRUNCH MUNCH
DINOSAUR LUNCH!

Paul Bright   Michael Terry

LITTLE TIGER
LONDON

Ty was big, and Ty was mean. He had a big, big mouth, with big, big jaws, and big, big teeth and big, big claws.

"Yeah! That's me," said Ty tyrannosaurus.

His roar echoed around the swamp
so that the other dinosaurs trembled
in their tummies.

Teri was small and Teri was sweet. She had a tiny, tiny mouth, with tiny, tiny jaws, and tiny, tiny teeth and tiny, tiny claws. And she loved her big brother more than any tyrannosaurus has ever been loved.

"Wuv oo, Ty rannynormus!"

gurgled Teri.

"Stay in your nest, pest," said Ty.
"I've got hunting to do."

Ty stomped through the swamp.
The ground sploshed and quaked and
quivered, and the dinosaurs heard
and shook and shivered.

"I'M HUNGRY!" roared Ty.

"I'M BIGGEST, I'M BADDEST,
AND I'M READY TO EAT.
I NEED SOME FRESH
STEGOSAURUS MEAT!"

He opened his big, big mouth and . . .

"Hug oo, Ty rannynormus!"
burbled Teri, wrapping her
arms around his huge leg.

Ty sighed as he saw his stegosaurus breakfast
paddle off through the swamp, snickering.
"You shouldn't be here, squirt!" he hissed.
"Get back to your drooling. Now stay away!"
And off he stomped, snorting.

Ty searched in the
swamp. The dinosaurs
ran and hid. They peered
through the reeds and peeked
from behind rocks. But it's not
easy to hide when you're a dinosaur.

"I'M STARVING!" roared Ty.

"I'M BIGGEST, I'M BADDEST,
AND I'M READY FOR LUNCH!
I NEED TRICERATOPS BONES
TO CRUNCH!"

He bared his big, big teeth and . . .

"Kiss oo, Ty rannynormus!"

slobbered Teri, planting
a wet, sloppy kiss on
his huge cheek.

Ty moaned as he saw his
triceratops lunch plodding
through the trees, laughing.

"You crawling, bawling bug!" he growled.
"Get back to your slurping and burping.
Now leave me alone!" And off he
stormed, snarling.

Ty crept through the swamp, quiet as quiet.
The other dinosaurs stayed still as still,
and even the leaves stopped rustling.
But a dinosaur can't stay still for long.
Ty heard a movement in the trees
and saw a long, long neck.

"I AM RAVENOUS!" roared Ty.
"I'M BIGGEST, I'M BADDEST,
AND I NEED A TREAT!
DIPLODOCUS STEAK LOOKS
TASTY TO EAT!"

He roared a big, big roar and . . .

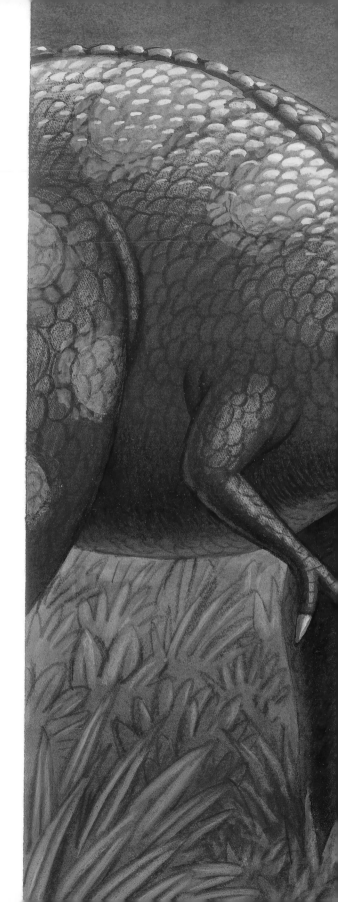

"Cuggle oo, Ty rannynormus!"
cooed Teri.

Ty groaned as his
diplodocus steak waddled
into the reeds, chuckling.

Ty stomped off through the swamp, then pounded
across the plain in a great temper. Teri watched him
getting further and further away. Then
she sat down in a heap and howled.

THUD! THUD! THUD!

Suddenly . . . the ground trembled.

"Ty rannynormus!" squeaked Teri.

But it wasn't.

IT WAS SPINOSAURUS!

Teri screamed. Spinosaurus was huge—
bigger even than her big brother Ty.
He had a huge, huge mouth, with
huge, huge teeth, and his
mouth was opening
wider and wider!

Ty roared and raged. He charged and chased.
And Spinosaurus turned and ran,
as fast as his lumbering
legs could go.

Then Ty reached down and scooped up Teri in his big, brotherly arms. He hugged his special, very annoying pest of a sister more tightly than any tyrannosaurus has ever been hugged.

"Wuv oo, Ty rannynormus,"

gurgled Teri.

"Wuv oo too, Teri rannynormus,"

said Ty, with a big, big smile.

"Now let's find some dinner!"